Presented to

Dalneigh Sunday
School, June 1994
Robert H. Nelson, Minister

Jesus said, "I am the way."
John 14:6

Printed in England

Visitor from Space

For Emily
Stephanie Jeffs

For Alison, Emma and Katie
Steve Hicks

Edited by David Martin

BIBLE SOCIETY
Stonehill Green, Westlea, SWINDON SN5 7DG, England

Published in association with AD Publishing Services Ltd
7 Hill Side, Cheddington, Leighton Buzzard, LU7 0SP

First published 1991

ISBN 0 564 08165 5

Printed in Hong Kong

Visitor from Space

Story by Stephanie Jeffs
Illustrated by Steve Hicks

'Greetings, Earthling!' said a voice from the Talksee computer.

Zorph ran towards it and pressed the green button marked SEE. Immediately a girl's face appeared on the screen.

'Hi, Zilla!' said Zorph as she pressed the red button marked TALK. 'How are you? It's great to see you!'

'I can't talk for long,' replied Zilla, 'I haven't many gold tokens left. But I've got a surprise for you. I'm coming to Earth, so get plenty of that lovely, crusty Earth-bread ready for me. Yum, I can almost smell it from here!'

'Of course I will, Zilla. But when are you coming?'

'I'll arrive... *beep, beep, beep...*'

Zilla's picture started to fade. Zorph rapidly pressed the green and red buttons, but it was no good, the picture had completely disappeared.

'Bother!' said Zorph.

'I'm sorry your call was discontinued, but the caller ran out of gold tokens,' said the Talksee computer.

'It's all very well saying you're sorry,' grumbled Zorph, wagging her finger at the computer. 'My best friend is coming all the way from Zilkon and I don't even know when she's arriving!'

'Sorry,' said the computer.

'Ha!' said Zorph and switched the computer off. The screen went blank. 'Serves you right!' said Zorph.

Zorph made her way to the kitchen and looked at the drawers of her Domestic Service Unit. She opened the drawer labelled TUESDAY TEA and took out a steaming plate of sausages in seaweed sauce with fresh vegetables. She started to eat, but it was far too hot, and so she sat back in her chair and went through the conversation with Zilla in her mind.

'No,' she thought, 'I've no idea what time she'll arrive, but the least I can do is have some fresh bread ready for her.'

She left her meal on the table and opened an unmarked kitchen drawer. Inside was a small keyboard and screen, and she typed in the words THREE LOAVES FRESH CRUSTY BROWN BREAD. HOLD.

Zorph returned to her meal. 'Whatever time Zilla does arrive,' she thought to herself, 'I'll have her favourite food waiting for her!'

Before she went to bed Zorph called her friend Una on the Talksee computer and told her all about Zilla's call.

'Well,' said Una, 'I'm glad she's coming, even if you don't know exactly when. I'm really looking forward to meeting her!'

'Yes,' said Zorph, 'we'll have to go out somewhere special and show her some good Earth sights. It'll be great fun. I can't wait!'

Zorph lay in her sleeping hammock and zipped her nightsleep cover around her. She closed her eyes and tried to sleep, but she was too excited. Eventually she reached for the switch above the hammock. As the Lullaby Screen lit up, her bedroom ceiling glowed with

the lights of the Milky Way. She stared at it, sighed and then pressed the switch again. Now the ceiling was full of fluffy, white clouds, drifting slowly in the wind. 'That's better!' thought Zorph, and within minutes she was in a deep sleep.

Zorph opened her eyes with a start. 'Bother!' she thought. Why had she woken up? She rolled over, desperately trying to go back to sleep. It was then she heard the chime of bells and realized there was a message on her Lullaby Screen. She rubbed her eyes and focused on the ceiling. FROM ZILLA TO ZORPH, she read, ARRIVING IN APPROXIMATELY FIVE MINUTES.

She shot out of bed, threw on some clothes and ran to the kitchen. She opened the unmarked kitchen drawer and typed in the words UNHOLD. Then she ran to the front door and opened it just as Zilla appeared around the corner of the walkway.

'Were you asleep?' asked Zilla, grinning. 'I chimed you because I didn't think you'd heard me say when I'd arrive. I must buy some more gold tokens. Sorry!'

'Never mind!' replied Zorph. 'I heard the most important bit – I've ordered some fresh, crusty Earth-bread for you. It should be ready now.'

'Great!' said Zilla, licking her lips. 'I've been looking forward to it. I'm starving!'

'Well, what are we waiting for?' said Zorph, leading her friend to the kitchen.

Zorph tapped DELIVER into the keyboard of her Domestic Service Unit then opened the drawer marked TUESDAY TEA with a flourish. 'Just as you like it!' she said proudly. The drawer was empty. 'Silly me,' she giggled. 'That got you worried. It must be after midnight, so it won't be in that drawer.'

Zorph reached for the drawer marked WEDNESDAY BREAKFAST and pulled it open.

Zilla looked inside. 'You always did like practical jokes!' she said as she picked up three dusty pieces of metal.

Zorph groaned. 'What's wrong with this machine?' she growled, giving the unit a kick. 'That doesn't look anything like bread.'

'No,' said Zilla, 'but it does look like dusty lead. Are you sure you typed in CRUSTY BREAD and not DUSTY LEAD? You never were very good at spelling!'

'Of course I'm sure!' said Zorph indignantly. 'Look for yourself!' She opened the unmarked drawer and there on the screen were the words THREE LOAVES FRESH CRUSTY BROWN BREAD DELIVERED.

'Well, it must be here somewhere,' said
Zilla. The two girls opened every drawer in the
kitchen, but in each one they found only three
pieces of dusty lead.

'Stupid machine!' snarled Zorph.

'Never mind,' said Zilla not very
convincingly.

Zorph looked at Zilla's disappointed face
and knew what to do.

'I'll call Una,' she said. 'She'll send us some
bread. Her machine will be working.'

'Are you sure she won't mind?' asked Zilla.
'It is rather late.'

'Of course she won't mind!' said Zorph.
'She's my friend, she'll be glad to help.'

Zorph switched on the Talksee computer
and tapped in Una's number. Within seconds
the word CONNECTING flashed on the screen.

'I'm sorry,' said the computer, 'Miss Una Unad is asleep and does not wish to be disturbed. If you wish to leave a message...'

'Don't bother!' muttered Zorph as she switched off the machine.

'It doesn't matter,' said Zilla.

'Of course it matters!' said Zorph. 'You're my best friend. You've travelled thousands of miles and you're hungry. Of course it matters! I'll chime her on her Lullaby Screen.'

Zorph and Zilla sat on the edge of the
sleeping hammock.

'Good,' said Zorph, 'she's got the Milky Way
display going. I never can get to sleep while
that's playing. I'll chime her now.' She pressed a
series of buttons on the small, portable
keyboard, and waited. Finally she flung it down
on the hammock in exasperation.

'What's the matter?' asked Zilla.

'She turned me off!' said Zorph. 'Cheek of it! She switched her Lullaby Screen to a different programme and turned off my message!'

'There's only one thing for it,' said Zorph. 'We'll go and see her.'

'It really doesn't matter...' said Zilla.

'I've made up my mind!' said Zorph, throwing Zilla an all-weather suit. 'She won't mind once she realizes why I want the bread. Anyway, she said she wanted to meet you.'

Zilla and Zorph stood outside Una's house in the cold evening air. The stars and planets shone out in the night sky, which was studded with the multi-coloured lights of rockets and space buses.

'Traffic's busy tonight,' said Zilla looking up at the sky.

Beep! A man on a hovercycle swerved past her, and Zilla toppled backwards. 'You OK?' asked Zorph, putting her arm round her friend. 'Be careful! Earth's full of mad drivers.'

'So I see,' muttered Zilla.

They walked together under the green glow of the safety street lamps. 'We'd better not take the shortcut,' said Zorph as they paused alongside a gap in the mega-buildings. 'It's safer to stay on the securipaths – even if it does take longer.'

Zorph rang the door bell with one hand,
and banged a small, brass door knocker with
the other.

'What *are* you doing?' asked Zilla in
disbelief.

'Una collects antiques,' explained Zorph.
'These are ancient ways of letting someone
know you want to see them. It's just as well
she's got them or we'd never have a hope of
waking her!'

'If Una doesn't wake up, someone else will.
What a noise!' said Zilla, covering her ears.

Zorph stopped and the two girls listened.
Silence.

'Never mind,' said Zilla, 'it doesn't matter. Maybe there's a night-store where we can get some...'

'I know she's here,' said Zorph lifting the door knocker. 'I'm sure she'll answer in a minute.'

After a few minutes they heard some sounds coming from inside Una's house. 'She's awake!' said Zorph triumphantly. 'You'll soon have your crusty Earth-bread, Zilla.'

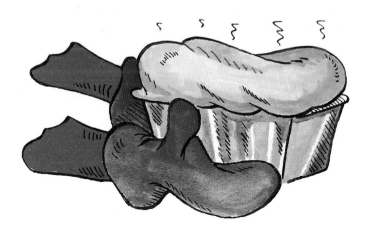

The front door slowly opened, and there stood Una, eyes half closed, still wrapped up in her sleeping duvet. She shuffled forwards.

'Una!' cried Zorph, 'I've been trying to call you!'

'I know,' mumbled Una sleepily, 'I heard – several times!'

'I'm sorry I've disturbed you,' said Zorph apologetically. 'As soon as we've gone you can go back to sleep.'

'No chance!' yawned Una as the smell of freshly baked bread wafted into the cold evening air.

'Mmm,' said Zilla and licked her lips.

'I'll see you tomorrow,' said Una. 'But now I've got to start baking. You see, earlier this evening I had a call on my TALKSEE computer. I've got a friend who lives in Zapron and she's coming to see me tomorrow. And guess what her favourite food is?!'

'Freshly baked Earth-bread?!' said Zilla and Zorph together.

Credits

Story by Stephanie Jeffs
Pictures by Steve Hicks
Based on something much older...

The Story Behind the Story

'Let me tell you a story.' Teachers, parents and older friends often say this when asked to explain something. If it's a good story it will use things we know about to help us understand something more difficult or more important. Sometimes the story will include a riddle or puzzle to help us think more carefully. Many famous teachers have used this idea. Often the stories are called parables. The word means 'putting things side by side'.

The story you have read is based on a parable Jesus told nearly 2000 years ago. Many of the parables told by Jesus have become very famous. He used these stories to help people think differently about things.

He told this story to people who prayed but were worried because God seemed very slow to answer.

And Jesus said to his disciples, 'Suppose one of you should go to a friend's house at midnight and say to him, "Friend, let me borrow three loaves of bread. A friend of mine who is on a journey has just come to my house, and I haven't got any food for him!" And suppose your friend should answer from inside, "Don't bother

*me! The door is already locked, and my children
and I are in bed. I can't get up and give you
anything." Well, what then? I tell you that even
if he will not get up and give you the bread
because you are his friend, yet he will get up and
give you everything you need because you are not
ashamed to keep on asking.'*

Luke 11:5-8

Things to Notice
About the Two Stories

The friend who was visited took some risks to
help their guest.

Waiting in the street in the dark for a long time
wasn't comfortable but it was rewarded.

When no reply was received, the friend who
wanted the bread must have felt like giving up
or going somewhere else.

It wasn't easy to give away the bread – some
more needed baking.

Thinking About It

'I've no idea what time she'll arrive, but the least I can do is have some fresh bread ready for her.'

❏ *Zorph is prepared to make a lot of effort to get what her friend wants. What does this show about their friendship?*

❏ *How do you show someone you are a friend?*

Zilla and Zorph stood outside Una's house in the cold evening air.

❏ *Zorph is prepared to take some risks to get what she wants. Have you ever wanted something that much?*

❏ *What sort of risks would you be willing to take?*

- *Can you think of any men or women who have taken really big risks to get what they wanted?*

- *Why do you think they have done this?*

- *Would you be prepared to take risks so that someone else might receive the benefits?*

Zorph rang the door bell with one hand, and banged a small, brass door knocker with the other.

- *At this stage it would have been easy to give up. However, Zorph wasn't the giving-up type! What does it take to be the type of person who never gives up?*

'I'm sorry I've disturbed you,' said Zorph apologetically. 'As soon as we've gone you can go back to sleep.'

'No chance!' yawned Una as the smell of freshly baked bread wafted into the cold evening air.

31

- *Zorph got what she wanted. How do you think she felt?*

- *How would Zilla feel when she eventually tasted the bread?*

- *Una had to give something away – it required sacrifice. What type of things would you sacrifice for your friends?*